Pony in the Schoolhouse

PONY
IN THE
SCHOOLHOUSE

by

MISKA MILES

Illustrated
by
Erik Blegvad

An Atlantic Monthly Press Book

BOSTON   Little, Brown and Company   TORONTO

By Miska Miles

KICKAPOO

DUSTY AND THE FIDDLERS

SEE A WHITE HORSE

PONY IN THE SCHOOLHOUSE

J
M

LIBRARY OF CONGRESS CATALOG CARD NO. 64–10179

FIRST EDITION

ATLANTIC–LITTLE, BROWN BOOKS
ARE PUBLISHED BY
LITTLE, BROWN AND COMPANY
IN ASSOCIATION WITH
THE ATLANTIC MONTHLY PRESS

Published simultaneously in Canada
by Little, Brown & Company (Canada) Limited

PRINTED IN THE UNITED STATES OF AMERICA

For Barbara Hort

1

Amy Ford hated Mondays for two reasons.

First of all, Mondays marked the beginning of five days when she and her brother Gordie had to walk two cactus-covered miles between farm and school.

And at school, there was always Rowdie Benson to spoil everything—eleven-year-old, freckle-faced Rowdie Benson.

"I hate walking to school," Amy said to her mother, "and when I get there, Rowdie Benson is always on the steps watching the road, and he yells at me. Things like: 'Look, here comes Red' —and he thinks he's very funny."

"I'd not pay any attention to him if I were you," Mama said. "The minute he finds out that you don't care, he won't bother you any more."

"I know," Amy said. "I try. But everyone laughs, and I can't help caring."

She looked at the barometer on the window sill. It was a little carved brown house with painted yellow roses climbing around the door, where two figures swung in and out, to say whether the day would be dark or fair—a man for sunshine and a wooden woman with an umbrella for storm. This morning, the little man and woman hesitated side by side, as though they couldn't decide whether the day would be fair or dreary.

Amy stood for a moment by the window. Beside the path, one poplar tree, bare except for a few leaves which still clung to its branches, pointed high toward the sky, and far beyond, past the road, a small band of wild horses clustered together on the range.

She looked for the small donkey that often

followed the horses, a donkey who belonged to no one, for he carried no brand.

She could see him shoving up toward the salt lick. "I wish I had that donkey," she said to herself. "He'd be better than no horse at all."

If she could only bring him in from the range, she and Gordie could ride to school, and half her troubles would be over.

Last year, Rowdie Benson and Rube Nichols brought him in. They looked funny, riding double, their long legs almost touching the ground. But the donkey had run away.

Mama was stirring batter for pancakes. She tested the griddle with a drop of water and the water sizzled and hopped. "Papa and Gordie ought to be about through with chores," she said.

Before Amy could reach the window to look, the door opened and there was Papa.

He stood waiting for Gordie.

"Here comes Pandemonium," Papa said pleasantly, as Gordie rushed into the kitchen.

"I smelled pancakes, so I hurried," Gordie announced in his loud, clear voice.

"I'm taking orders," Mama said. "How many?"

"Oh, about forty-seven," Gordie answered.

"I'll have three, please, Mama," Amy said.

"I have three ready," Mama said. "Gordie can wait. He eats faster than anyone else, anyhow. I'll serve your father next. Drink your milk while you wait, Gordie. Do you want six?"

"Yes, ma'am." Gordie drank his milk.

"The donkey's out near the salt lick with the range horses," Amy said.

"Why don't we catch him, like Rowdie and Rube did?" Gordie asked.

"No use going on foot," his father said. "You'd scare the wild horses and the donkey would be right with them."

"I know," Amy said. "When Rowdie caught him, the donkey had come up to the salt lick by himself, and Rowdie rode out to bring him in. If I ONLY had a horse."

Papa smiled. "If you had a horse, you wouldn't need the donkey. I'm sorry we don't have one you can use, but walking really doesn't hurt anyone. I know it's a long way—"

Amy didn't say anything, but she truly didn't like walking in winter. Soon snow would lie heavy over the fields and white drifts would fill the hollows.

"Besides," Gordie said, "Amy doesn't want just any pony. She only wants old Star."

"I do not," Amy said. "Star belongs to Mrs. Pettiboy, and I don't want anything that belongs to somebody else."

"Well, anyway, she likes old Star better than any other horse," Gordie explained to his parents. "You see, old Star grabs Amy's fur cap right off her head. Old Star doesn't want Amy to leave the barnyard. Mrs. Pettiboy says so."

Amy laughed. "Star likes me." She thought about Star. Perhaps Mrs. Pettiboy would let her borrow Star long enough to bring in the donkey. . . .

Papa finished eating first and pushed back from the table. He let his hand fall on Gordie's shoulder. "You behave yourself today," he said. "Mind your sister. Do you hear?"

"I hear," Gordie said.

When Papa opened the door, a gust of cold wind blew across the room and Amy shivered. She finished her breakfast and hurried to get ready for school.

The telephone rang and she could hear Mama talking.

"They haven't started yet. . . . Of course they will. . . . She doesn't mind at all. . . . You're welcome."

9

She hung up the receiver. "That was Mrs. Pettiboy. She needs you. I said you'd drop by."

Often Mrs. Pettiboy telephoned and asked her to stop by on the way to school to help with Star, for Mrs. Pettiboy's rheumatism and winter seemed to arrive at about the same time.

"She'll want us to feed old Star," Gordie said.

Amy felt pleased at the way things were turning out this morning. Maybe she might even ask Mrs. Pettiboy about borrowing Star. If she could get the donkey off the range, life would be wonderful. But then she remembered Rowdie. Life would almost be wonderful.

She twisted a woolen scarf around her neck and picked up her lunch bucket.

"I'm ready" she said. "Where's Gordie?"

2

It was a long road that led to Mrs. Pettiboy's.
They trudged up the slow rise of the first hill,
covered with cactus and prairie dog holes, with
Pikes Peak far away on the edge of everything.

She leaned against the wind and felt it sharp
against her face. Gordie's nose was cranberry-red
when they finally turned in at Mrs. Pettiboy's place.

"I like helping Mrs. Pettiboy," Gordie said.

"Helping?" Amy looked at him. "And where
are you while I feed old Star? In the house, eating Mrs. Pettiboy's cookies."

Star was standing down in the barnyard looking at them solemnly.

"Why does everybody call her old Star?" Gordie asked.

"Well, she's old," Amy said. "She's too old to work."

Mrs. Pettiboy must have seen them coming, because she opened the door as they went up the path. "Amy," she called, "when you've fed Star, come on in the house. I made gingerbread yesterday."

As Amy started toward the barnyard, she heard Gordie ask, "How old is Star, Mrs. Pettiboy?"

And Mrs. Pettiboy answered, "She's twenty-three if she's a day. And that's old for a horse."

"That's old for anything," Gordie said.

Star didn't seem old. Her coat was as golden as dark honey, and it shone like silk.

"You're beautiful," Amy said, "and I wish you were mine. I'm going to ask Mrs. Pettiboy if I can borrow you for just one ride. We'll get that donkey, and you'd like to go, wouldn't you?"

Star tossed her head and snatched Amy's cap. Amy threw an arm around the pony's neck and

reached for it. Laughing, she pushed it into
her pocket.

Star shoved against her shoulders. After Amy
forked hay into the manger, she hurried to the
house. Gordie had gingerbread crumbs from one
ear to the other.

"Mrs. Pettiboy," Amy said, "I'm going to try
to bring the donkey in off the range. You know,
the donkey that trails the horses?"

Mrs. Pettiboy nodded.

"I can't catch him if I'm on foot, but I think I
can get him if I ride out for him, and I've been

wondering if you'd let me borrow Star to bring him in."

"Nobody's been on Star for the last two years," Mrs. Pettiboy said, "but I'm sure you could manage her. There's no use trying to catch the donkey when he's with the horses, though. Scare the bunch, and you scare the donkey."

"I know," Amy said. "I thought I'd wait until he comes to the salt lick by himself."

"When he does, you come for Star," Mrs. Pettiboy said. "I'll be glad to lend her."

With gingerbread added to their lunch pails, Amy and Gordie set out for school.

Down the second slope, the road led past the church.

"I'm always glad when we get this far," Amy said, "because we're halfway."

14

They went on, up the next hill. Gordie pointed to the cemetery. "And I'm always glad when we get to the graveyard, because here, we're MORE than halfway."

The wind bent the sparse weeds that grew over the graves, and the tombstones made quiet gray shadows on the earth.

Below, in the distance, was the schoolhouse, its roof steeply pointed for shedding the heavy snows. White smoke curled up from its chimney, which meant that Miss Grace was sitting at her desk, getting ready to hear the youngest read, or writing a lesson on the blackboard for the older ones.

The woodbox would be heaped high with

kindling for burning in the stove that stood fat
and important in the center of the room. And today, they would all shove their desks close to
its red glow.

Amy thought about winter and snows—

When Miss Grace first came to teach, Papa

16

took her over to see the schoolhouse and Amy went along.

"We have to be ready for blizzards in this part of Colorado," he said. "It's a good idea to keep the woodbox full. You'll notice that the desks aren't fastened to the floor. If there should be a blizzard you'd all have to stay here until someone was able to get through to you. And if you run out of wood, there are the desks to burn."

He opened the door of a small closet at the back of the room.

"Here's where we keep the emergency equipment," he said. "The biggest danger of fire out here would be if a spark from the chimney caught on the roof. This rope—" he pointed to a coil of heavy rope—"this would reach over the roof, and the big boys wouldn't have any trouble hauling themselves up with a bucket of water to put out a fire. Here are the buckets. And here's the ax—and there on the shelf is a lamp, and here on the floor a can of kerosene, and you're ready for anything."

When Miss Grace asked how she would know a blizzard if it came, Papa said:

"Look out the window. Look for the hitching rail. If you can't see it for the snowing, then you can be sure it's a blizzard."

Amy and Gordie went down the hill.

Gordie swung his lunch pail over his head, around and around in circles.

Two of the younger girls were standing on the schoolhouse steps, but Rowdie Benson was not in sight.

3

Rowdie's spotted pony wasn't tied to the hitching rail, and Amy drew a big breath of relief as they crossed to the schoolhouse.

Gordie went up the steps in one leap.

Miss Grace was sitting at her desk looking happy, and Amy wished that she could always feel the way Miss Grace looked on Monday mornings. She looked as if she knew something nice would happen. Her brown eyes sparkled and a smile curled the corners of her mouth.

The room was warm and pleasant and everything was wonderful.

But suddenly someone was galloping hard down the road. Hoofbeats thudded against the earth, coming closer and closer, and she knew it had to be Rowdie.

And there he was, coming lickety-split, headed straight for the schoolhouse. He pulled his pony to a sliding stop. Then, in a whirl of dust, he rode right up the steps to the open door.

Miss Grace screamed: "Watch out!"

He rode into the schoolhouse.

"Rowdie Benson," Miss Grace said. "Get that pony out of here this minute. This very minute. Do you hear me?"

Rowdie edged his pony around. "See how he turns. He doesn't even touch a desk. This is a stunt. I've been practicing here on Saturdays."

He started down the steps, the pony sidling carefully, feeling his way.

Rowdie called over his shoulder: "I saw this in the moving-picture house in town. A cowboy rode right up the courthouse steps and into the courthouse."

Miss Grace didn't say anything, but her face was very red. She tapped the bell hard and the morning classes started.

At recess, Amy hurried outside. She joined the smaller girls who were standing near Rowdie's pony, and then Rowdie appeared.

"Redhead, Gingerbread," he taunted. "Five cents a loaf."

Her cheeks felt hot as fire, and she thought to herself: Don't answer. Don't pay any attention to him. Don't say a word—

He reached out and gave her braid a pull, laughing loudly.

Something in Amy exploded. Like a bobcat she started after him.

Arms flew and fists pounded.

"Hit him again, Amy," someone was yelling.

And then Amy heard another voice.

"*Rowdie.*" It was Miss Grace. "What has come over you today? And *Amy*, I can't believe this of you. Inside the schoolhouse. To your desks. Both of you. Immediately."

"Want me to hit him for you, Amy?" Gordie looked hopeful.

"Gordie," Miss Grace said. "Inside for you, too."

"But I haven't done anything yet, Miss Grace," Gordie said.

Miss Grace pointed to the schoolhouse. "IN."

When Amy reached her desk, she was warm with love for Gordie, and she put her face down in her arms. She would not cry. She would not. Her face pressed against the cool smoothness of the desk, and she thought how much she hated Rowdie Benson.

4

Morning seemed long. At last it was lunchtime.

"My pie is mixed with my egg sandwich," Gordie said. "It's a new kind of stew. Eggberry stew. Understand the joke? Eggs and blackberry pie. Eggberry."

"I understand." Amy was glad that Gordie was in her family.

When school was dismissed that afternoon, they started up the road toward home, and Rowdie Benson circled around them at a gallop, whooping like an Indian. He stopped shouting long enough to call: "Hi, Red, want a ride?"

"I do not." Amy knew that she would walk

a million miles rather than ride with Rowdie.

As he galloped away, she looked straight ahead toward the top of the hill, where the road seemed to end against the sky.

Finally she reached the top, and the prairie stretched on and on without end, and the sky covered it over like a gray bowl. And at long last, there was home.

Beside the path, the poplar tree dropped a brown leaf, a leaf of winter. It fell to the ground like a wounded bird, and Amy picked it up.

The color was lovely and soft and almost the shade of her mother's wedding ring. It reminded her of something else, but she couldn't think what. She turned it over, and then she knew.

She pulled a braid forward and held the leaf beside it. They were the same color—hair and leaf.

Why, she thought, my hair isn't red. It isn't really red at all. It's the same color as the leaf—the brown, brown leaf. If I had a brown dress, everyone would see that my hair is brown—brown—brown. . . .

Inside the kitchen, the tall clock ticked in the corner and the kettle sputtered on the stove. Home was warm and welcoming.

Gordie plunged in behind her and went straight to the cookie jar.

Amy held out the leaf to show her mother.

"This is brown, isn't it?" she asked.

"Yes, it is." Her mother waited.

Gordie looked too. "It's brown all right. Anybody can see that."

Amy held it beside her braid. "My hair and the leaf are the same color. Mama, do you think I could have a brown dress?" Anxiously, Amy watched her mother's face.

Her mother held out her hand for the leaf.

"It's beautiful," she said. "The color would be nice on you, nice for winter. If you want it specially, we might order the material now. You could help make it."

That night after dinner, they looked at the mail-order catalogue. Amy looked for dress goods.

"I'll put the leaf in with the order," she said. "Then they'll know exactly what I want."

"Don't lick that envelope," Gordie said. "Maybe I can have something too."

He thumbed through the catalogue.

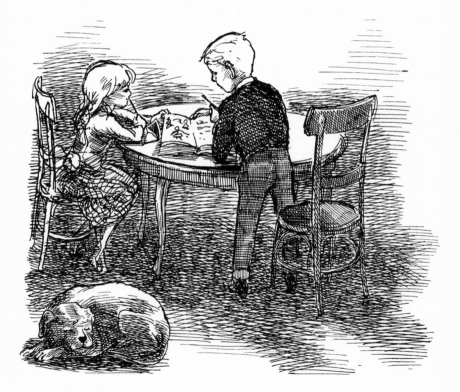

"If she has a dress, could I have snowshoes?
I could walk right over the schoolhouse if the
snow drifts enough. Look. Could I have a jackknife? Five blades. Boy, that would come in

handy." Rapidly, he flipped the pages. "What
about a saddle? Here's one trimmed with silver."

Amy giggled. "What would you put a saddle on?"

"Ask your father about the jackknife," his mother said.

"Papa. Can I have a jackknife? Look. Five blades."

His father looked over Gordie's shoulder. "Did you behave yourself in school today?"

Gordie looked at Amy. "Yep," he said.

His father smiled. "Whatever your mother says—"

Gordie hunched his shoulders and waited.

His mother looked at him a minute. "Perhaps it's time you had a good knife."

Gordie's smile spread almost from one ear to the other. But Amy thought about the brown dress. Even Rowdie would see that her hair was the color of the dress, leaf brown—not red.

Outside, the wind howled and the kitchen felt

cozy and small, like a safe-lighted cave, deep in
a flat empty world.

The week seemed long. Each night when they
reached home, Amy asked about the mail.

When Friday came at last, the package from
the mail-order house was there waiting.

Amy took off the wrapping. Gordie's knife
was on top, rolled in yellow tissue paper. She
opened her own package and looked at the fabric.

It was green and black plaid. It wasn't brown.

She took one long look at it, and put her head
in her arms and sobbed.

"Oh, Amy darling," Mama said. "A dress isn't
that important. Really it isn't."

Mama touched her shoulder, and Amy cried
harder than ever. Mama didn't understand.

"Please don't cry, Amy—"

"I can't help it, Mama. You see, this was to be
—a dress—a very special dress—for a reason—"

"I know," said Mama.

Amy wondered if Mama really did know, and
after a while she was able to lift her head and
wipe her face on a handkerchief.

Gordie had unwrapped his knife and was
sneaking from the kitchen. The back of his
neck was flag-red.

Amy stiffened. "Mama. Look at Gordie. He's
guilty about something—GORDIE!"

5

Gordie made a dash for his room, and Amy was right after him. She grabbed his shirt.

"I haven't done anything. It was only something I didn't do."

"What do you mean?" Amy shook him. "What was it?"

"Well, a letter came from the store people—"

"Mama. He didn't give me my mail. Mama!" She shook him again. "Where is my letter? What did you do with it?"

He reached in his pocket. He took out a ball of string, three marbles, a short pencil and finally a crumpled, dirty envelope.

Amy grabbed it. "It's addressed to me, and he didn't give it to me." She opened it and read:

"'We do not have the brown material in stock. We can substitute a plaid in the same fine quality and at the same price. If this is not satisfactory will you let us know at once?' Why didn't you give me my letter? I would have waited—"

"I forgot," Gordie said.

"Gordie," Mama said, "I think you owe your sister an apology."

"I'm sorry," Gordie said. He looked as though he might cry, too.

Mama rubbed the cloth between her fingers. "The quality is nice," she said. "And it IS pretty."

Amy sniffed.

"We could cut it out this evening," Mama said. "We could make it together—"

Gordie slipped out of the room.

When Amy awakened the next morning under her pile of soft quilts, she stretched as far as she could reach. The sheets were like ice, and she huddled back in the warm spot where she had slept.

She could hear Gordie's voice.

"There's snow everywhere. Look. I never saw so much snow."

She jumped out of bed, and dressed as quickly as she could. Outside her window, the world lay blinding bright in the morning sun. She could see Papa, already clearing a path to the barn.

After breakfast, Mama laid the dress pieces on the kitchen table. "We'll let everything else go," she said, "and we'll finish the dress."

6

The dress was finished. She wore it to church. It was a plain dress with pleats and a round collar, and there were two pockets hidden in the pleats.

I would have liked this a lot, Amy thought to herself, except for wanting the brown.

That afternoon, the telephone jingled. Gordie answered. "For you, Amy," he called.

Amy took the receiver. "Hello?"

Mrs. Pettiboy's voice came over the wire.

"Amy, I've been thinking a lot about you and old Star. So often I have to ask if you'll stop by and feed her. I know she's too old to work, but she just might not be too old to go to school. Now if your father wants to feed her, you can have her to ride to school. You can keep her in your barn."

"You mean to keep?" Amy asked. She drew a big breath.

"Ask your father," Mrs. Pettiboy said.

"He's right here, Mrs. Pettiboy." Amy turned to her father.

"Papa. Mrs. Pettiboy says we can have Star if we'll feed her, and Gordie and I can ride her to school. She wants to know if it's all right—"

Papa leaned back in his chair. "Well—" Would Papa never answer?—"I understand from Gordie that you like old Star better than any horse in the country. You tell Mrs. Pettiboy that we'll make a bargain. When Star gets too old to go to school, we'll turn her out to spend her days in a good green pasture, and we'll give her a warm barn to sleep in, nights."

Amy thought she couldn't breathe. Her heart turned a flip. She spoke into the phone. "Mrs.

Pettiboy? It's all right. We'll keep Star and give her a good home all her life."

"Then Star is yours, Amy. You can stop for her on your way to school tomorrow."

"Oh we will, Mrs. Pettiboy. This will be the nicest Monday of my whole life." Amy wanted to say a million things, but her heart was so full, she could only say, "Thank you."

She hung up the phone and turned to face her family. "Star is mine," she said.

"WHEEEEEEE," Gordie said. "Old Star will like that. I'll bet it's been pretty dull in Mrs. Pettiboy's barnyard. She'll like it at school."

Amy started to shake. She had never been so

excited in her life. This was a million times better than getting the donkey. She gave Gordie a hug.

"Do you want to ride to school with me, or shall we get the donkey for you?"

"I'll ride with you on old Star," Gordie answered. "Gee, I hope we don't get snowed in tomorrow morning. Does anybody think it looks like more snow?"

On the window sill, the wooden woman was still outside the little brown house, her umbrella raised for bad weather.

The next morning, when she got ready for school, Amy put on the new dress. She shoved her hands in the pockets. It was really a nice dress, and this was a wonderful Monday morning.

They hurried faster than usual.

The weather was so cold that Amy's breath rose up from her gray scarf and froze on her eyelashes.

Mrs. Pettiboy was waiting for them.

"I almost telephoned you not to come," she

said. "Old Star wandered off early this morning. She hasn't done that for years. Afterward, I was glad I hadn't telephoned, because I've got that donkey you wanted, instead."

Amy couldn't remember when so many disappointments had stacked up in a heap.

"I left the barnyard gate open," Mrs. Pettiboy said, "because I thought Star might change her mind and decide to turn around and come back—but when that donkey trotted in, I hurried out and shut the gate. Since Star's gone, I knew you'd be glad to have him."

"Good old donkey," Gordie said. "I don't care what I ride as long as I ride."

"I care," Amy said unhappily.

They walked toward the barn.

"That donkey's got a mean look in his eye," Gordie said. "I'll bet he's planning to clear out already."

"I agree," Mrs. Pettiboy said. "I don't trust him. Look at his ears. Gordie, you run in the barn and get Star's bridle. It's hanging by the stall. It

will be a little big for him, but it will do as well as anything."

"Mrs. Pettiboy," Amy said. "Will Star come back?"

"When she gets ready, she'll come trotting home. In fact, I'll be surprised if she isn't back today. It looks like more snow."

Amy was almost afraid to ask the question in her mind.

"When Star comes back, do you still want us to take her home?"

"Certainly. We made a bargain. Star's yours."

The donkey's eyes were too bright. His eyelashes were long and curling and his fur was rough and thick. He stood quietly while Amy slipped the bridle over his head and slid onto his back.

"Hop up behind me, Gordie. Here's my hand. Good."

Mrs. Pettiboy opened the gate.

"Don't forget," she said. "Star's yours."

40

"I couldn't forget, Mrs. Pettiboy," Amy said. "I couldn't forget in a million years."

As they rode down the hill, the first snowflakes drifted down slowly, and then fell faster. The donkey jogged and snorted and twitched as though he were trying to get rid of Gordie and Amy.

They jounced along fast—faster. They passed the church.

"We're halfway," Amy said.

On they went. They were almost past the cemetery. "We're more than halfway," Gordie said. "WAIT. LOOK. STOP. LOOK IN THE GRAVEYARD. THERE'S A HORSE'S GHOST THERE—"

For a second, Amy was afraid to look.

"Silly," she said. "That's not a ghost. That's Star."

She pulled the donkey up short. Together they hauled at the rein to turn him.

Finally, he turned his neck, but he refused to move his body.

"Give me your lunch pail," Amy said. "You'll just have to slide off and push."

Gordie slipped over the donkey's tail and started pushing.

"Watch out," Amy shouted. "He's flattened his ears."

Gordie dodged as the donkey kicked out with his heels, and Amy almost went over his head.

"I'm getting off too," Amy said. "I'm going to get Star." She slid to the ground. "Gordie, you'll have to hang on to the donkey, because I'm going to take the bridle. HURRY. Put your arms around his neck and hang on. Talk to him."

"What'll I say?" Gordie asked.

Amy could have shaken him. "What'll you say? Say something nice." She started for the cemetery, the bridle in her hand.

Star stood quietly, waiting, watching through the snow.

"It's Amy. You know me, Star. Dear Star."

Star backed away and slowly circled the cemetery. When she reached the road, she broke into a trot. As she passed the donkey, he joined her, galloping close behind.

"The donkey wouldn't listen," Gordie said. "I had to let go."

Amy watched sadly as the pony and donkey headed down the hill at a gallop toward the schoolhouse. "Look where we'd be if we were riding."

"We'd be almost there," Gordie said.

Far ahead, Amy saw Rowdie getting out of the Benson jeep. Then it chugged off in a flurry of snow.

Amy wished she could hide the bridle. She

looked around, but there was no place to leave it.

With reluctant steps, she crossed to the school-house. Rowdie was there waiting.

"Look," he shouted. "LOOK AT RED. Here comes a cowgirl without a horse. LOOK AT RED. She's got a bridle and nothing to put it on. Get a horse. Get a horse."

Gordie joined in the laughing. "That's funny," he said.

"Very, very funny." Amy didn't smile.

At recess, the wind whipped up a gale, and the children stayed inside the schoolroom close to the stove.

Gordie stood at the window. "It's snowing real hard, Miss Grace," he said happily.

He was right. Snow was falling thick and fast.

As Miss Grace reached for the bell, Gordie looked at his desk, and Amy knew what he was thinking. He was hoping that there would be a blizzard, and that they would have to split up the desks for burning.

"Gordie Ford," she said, "if you so much as mention the ax, I'll hit you."

"Okay," Gordie answered pleasantly. "I won't mention it."

7

They all stayed inside the schoolhouse at lunchtime. Amy's apple pie was shaken up a bit, but her ham sandwich was whole, and everything tasted good, down to the last crumb.

"I've got a mixed-up lunch again," Gordie said. "Hamapple stew."

They had finished eating and had set their lunch pails on a bench at the back of the room, when a shadow fell across the window by Miss Grace's desk.

"It's old Star," Gordie yelled.

Amy ran to the window. "It IS Star," she said. She turned to Miss Grace. "Miss Grace, it's Mrs.

Pettiboy's Star, and I'm watching for her, and I'm supposed to catch her—that is, she isn't really Mrs. Pettiboy's Star—" Amy ran and snatched the bridle from the hook beside the door.

"Old Star's ours now," Gordie said importantly as he opened the door.

Gordie reached Star first and knotted his fingers in her mane, while Amy slipped the bridle over her head.

They led her to the hitching rail.

Rube Nichols carried kindling and wood from the shed behind the schoolhouse and filled the woodbox in the corner of the room.

Amy walked to the window where she could see Star. Star stood there patiently, head lowered, tail toward the wind, safe, waiting—

The afternoon grew dark and cold. Everyone shifted about uneasily and no one could remember lessons. Finally, Miss Grace gave up, and they all pushed their desks closer to the fire and listened while she told stories about happy things.

At last it was time to go home. When Miss Grace rang the bell, Rowdie walked to the window.

"Do you know, Miss Grace," he said, "I think this is a blizzard."

"What makes you think so?" she asked.

"See that hill out there?" He pointed.

"Well, no," she said. "I can't really see it."

"That's what I mean," Rowdie said. "If this keeps up we won't be able to see anything in a few minutes."

Amy looked at the hitching rail. She could hardly see old Star standing there, unmoving—

"I guess we'll have to stay here," Miss Grace said. Her voice sounded loud. "We'll stay right here until someone calls for us. This is fun. We are pioneers. Let's look in our lunch pails and see what we can find for our supper."

"No use looking in mine," Gordie said. "I ate everything at noon."

48

Amy couldn't remember seeing a real blizzard. She and Gordie had heard stories about the last one, when Rube Nichols's grandfather had to spend two nights and two days in his barn, because the blizzard came up while he was doing the milking. He couldn't see his house at all, and he didn't dare start out to find it, for everyone in the country knew that with nothing to guide you, you might wander in circles until you finally lay down in the snow to sleep and to die.

Amy walked to the window and looked outside. The snow closed in against the window and she couldn't see the hitching rail. She couldn't see anything at all, neither earth nor sky. She could only hear the wind as it beat against the windows. And Star was out there—

"Miss Grace," Amy said. "I can't see the hitching rail. I have to get Star."

"Amy, if you can't see the rail, this is a blizzard," Miss Grace said. "I can't let you leave the schoolhouse. You'd never find your way back. I'm sorry. You can't go."

Old Star would be standing out there, her tail turned toward the wind, her head hanging, and Amy knew that old Star would stand there until she froze to death.

She brushed tears away with the back of her hand. "Miss Grace—"

Rowdie Benson spoke up. "Look, Miss Grace. Red is right. We ought to get that old pony inside. She'd probably never last through a blizzard, standing out there all alone. I can get her in. Wait. Let me show you."

He opened the door to the closet and hauled out the coil of rope. "This reaches over the roof. It'll reach from here to the hitching rail. I'll tie one end around my waist, and you can hang on to the other end here. I'll go out at the end of it, and I'll find that hitching rail. There's nothing to it, Miss Grace. I couldn't get lost. LOOK. You'll have this end. You and Rube can haul me back in, any minute you want to."

Miss Grace hesitated, and Amy could see that she was weakening.

"That old pony will stand there and die," Rowdie said.

That did it.

Miss Grace looked carefully at the knot at Rowdie's waist.

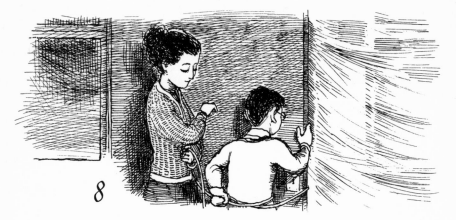

8

"I'll give this knot another loop or two, just to be sure it can't possibly come loose," Miss Grace said. She gave it a tug. "There. We'll unroll the coil as you go. I'll give you exactly ten minutes, Rowdie, and not a second more. If you're not back then, we're going to pull you in. Understand?"

Miss Grace looked at her watch. "Five minutes past five," she said.

They opened the door and Rowdie edged outside, crouched against the wind. Immediately he disappeared in the whiteness.

Rube held the door ajar just enough to let the rope pass through.

Time moved slowly. And then the rope was taut.

"He's at the end of the rope now," Rube said.

Slowly the rope swung to the left, then after a time to the right.

Amy thought of Rowdie out there in the blizzard, hunting through the snow—reaching for Star.

At twelve minutes after five o'clock, the rope went slack.

"I think he's coming in," Miss Grace said. "Rube! Gordie! Take hold of the rope as I pull it in."

There was no sound from the whiteness outside except the crying of the wind. Then, there was Rowdie, coming out of the snow, trying to smile, and behind him, Star's head and shoulders —her forelegs. . . .

Miss Grace held the door wide. "Bring her in."

The old pony stumbled as Rowdie led her up the steps.

Amy shoved desks, and then Star was in a

corner, blowing through her bridle, steam rising from her sides as she looked around on the floor for hay. Amy rubbed her down with her scarf and talked to her softly.

Rowdie was as close to the big stove as he could get without being scorched. His teeth were chattering. He fumbled at the stiff, frozen rope.

Gordie opened the longest blade of his knife.

"It will take a good knife to cut that rope off," he said.

After they settled down, Miss Grace dusted the little kerosene lamp and lit it and started to read to them. For a long while, she read their favorites, stories and poems that they liked to hear over and over again. Star stamped and whinnied softly, and moved closer to Amy.

The little lamp threw a circle of light in the dark room, and still it stormed.

"Woodbox is empty, Miss Grace," Gordie said cheerfully.

"I see," Miss Grace said. "All right, Rube, I guess it's time to get the ax."

9

Rube brought out the ax.

"Here, take my desk," Gordie said. "I've got it ready. I emptied it. I even took out the ink-well."

Rube laid Gordie's desk across the woodbox and lifted the ax.

The desk split neatly in two. The ax fell again and again, and soon there was a pile of oak in the woodbox.

"Let me help." Gordie lifted the lid of the stove and dropped in the first piece.

The fire crackled and roared and the air was sharp with burning varnish.

Old Star stamped her foot and whinnied.

Miss Grace laughed. "I never thought I'd see the day when I'd invite a pony into my schoolroom—"

"Or burn up the desks," Gordie added.

Amy had a strange and prickly feeling. Suppose it snowed so hard and so long that no one could get through. Suppose Rube split up all the desks and burned them one by one, and suppose it grew colder and colder. . . .

Rube was cracking the second desk apart when Miss Grace stopped him.

"Listen," she said.

"Maybe it's our jeep," Rowdie said. "I think my father can get through all right. I think he'll make it if he follows the ridges."

Miss Grace opened the door a crack and waited. Sure enough, there was a chugging sound and two beams of light shone through the falling snow, and the jeep nosed right up to the steps.

"Are you all there?" Mr. Benson called.

56

"We're here and we're all right," Miss Grace answered.

"Thank God for that," he said. He came into the schoolhouse with a gust of snow and wind, and when he saw old Star looking at him from her corner, he started to laugh. He laughed so hard that he had to wipe his eyes and blow his nose.

"Bundle up," he said. "All of you. The wind's let up a bit and the snow's lighter. We won't have any trouble getting through to our place. Your folks will pick you up there."

When he led Star outside to tie her to the jeep, she shoved at his shoulders.

"The pony's hungry," he said.

"So am I." Gordie's voice was loud and good-natured. "I've never been so hungry before."

"Well, hurry and pile in. You won't be hungry for long."

Amy jumped in back where she could keep an eye on Star.

"Don't worry about the pony," Mr. Benson

said. "At the rate we'll travel, she'll probably run over US."

They piled into the jeep, the bigger boys and girls crowded in back with Miss Grace, and the smaller in front with Mr. Benson.

All of us and Star, Amy thought happily.

The Fords' spring wagon was tied up at the Bensons'.

Gordie hopped over the side of the jeep with a shout, and Amy heard Papa's voice from inside the house.

"Well, here's Pandemonium. Where's Amy?"

Mrs. Benson bustled around giving everyone hot cocoa and bread and butter. "This will hold you until you get home," she said.

10

The next morning, the little man in the barometer swung outside, and fair weather had come
again.

Amy couldn't wait to get out to feed Star.

Gordie came rushing into the barn. "You'll
have to hurry or we'll be late for school," he said.
"Mama said so."

After breakfast, they bridled Star, and Gordie
led her to the porch, where he and Amy could
slide over onto her bare back.

They started down the path toward the road,
rocking along with the swing of the old pony's
back.

"She's an easy rider," Amy said.

"Easiest in the world," Gordie agreed.

As they neared Mrs. Pettiboy's farm, they heard a familiar bray. There in the Pettiboy barn door stood the donkey, and he turned his head to watch as they passed by.

"Smart donkey," said Gordie. "He knows where to go when it storms."

Then they dipped down the last slope toward the schoolhouse, and Amy saw Rube Nichols and Rowdie Benson on the steps.

Rowdie was yelling, "Hi, Red!"

Suddenly it didn't matter that he called her Red. Happily, she patted Star's neck. Everything was right in Amy's world.

Date Due

JY 28 65			
MA 31 67			
OC 2 68			
FE 21 '74			
FEB 1			
FEB 15 '78			
APR 07 '79			
APR 23 '81			
FEB 22 '82			